THIS WALKER BOOK BELONGS TO:

_____

For my mother and father

First published 1994
by Walker Books Ltd
87 Vauxhall Walk
London SE11 5HJ

This edition published 1995

2 4 6 8 10 9 7 5 3 1

© 1994 Inga Moore

This book has been typeset in Garamond.

Printed in Hong Kong

British Library Cataloguing in Publication Data
A catalogue record for this book is
available from the British Library.
ISBN 0-7445-3626-X

A BIG DAY FOR Little Jack

Inga Moore

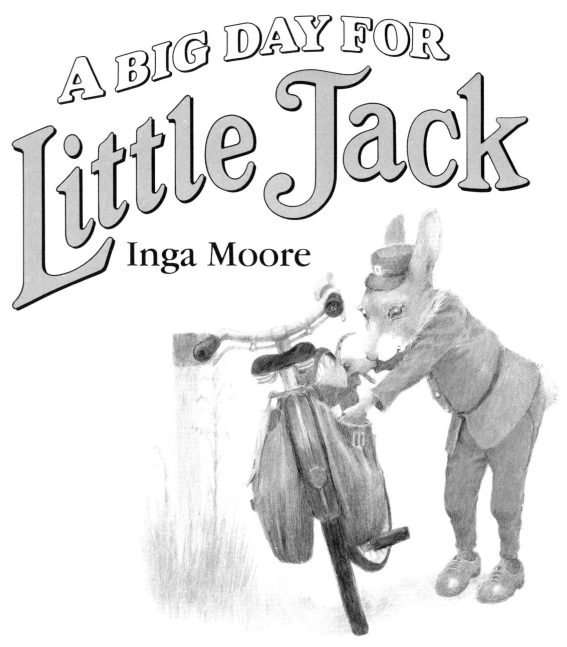

WALKER BOOKS
AND SUBSIDIARIES

LONDON • BOSTON • SYDNEY

One day the postman brought a card
for Little Jack Rabbit.

Mummy read it out. It said,
"You are invited to a party."
Little Jack Rabbit had never
been to a party before.
"Will you come with me?"
he asked.
"Mummies aren't invited,
Little Jack," said
Mummy.

Little Jack Rabbit went shopping with Daddy. They bought a present for Little Jack to take to the party and some new shoes for him to wear.

"Now we will buy you a jacket," said Daddy. "You must look smart if you are going to a party." Little Jack Rabbit had never been to a party before. He had never had to look smart. "Will *you* come with me?" he asked. "Will *you* come to the party?" "Daddies aren't invited, Little Jack," said Daddy.

At home Little Jack Rabbit's sisters Nancy, Rhona
and Rita wrapped up the present in some blue and
white striped paper. "Don't forget to take it to the
party, Little Jack," said Nancy.

Little Jack Rabbit had never been to a party before.
He had never had to look smart and he had never
taken a present.

"Will *you* come with me?" he asked.

"Big sisters aren't invited, Little Jack," said Nancy.

Before the party Little Jack Rabbit's big brother
Buck gave him a hot soapy bath. Buck had been to
lots of parties.
"What are parties like?" asked Little Jack.
"You'll play party games," said Buck, "and make
new friends."
Little Jack Rabbit had never been to a party before.
He had never had to look smart
and he had never taken a
present. He had *never*
played party games or
made new friends.
"Will *you* come with
me?" he asked.
"Big brothers aren't
invited, Little Jack,"
said Buck.

Granpa had been mending
a toy for Little Jack Rabbit.
It was Little Jack's favourite
toy, Bunnikin.
"Why aren't you ready,
Little Jack?" Granpa asked.
"You will be late for the
party."
"I don't want to go," said
Little Jack Rabbit.
"Why not?" asked Granpa.
"I don't want to go
on my own," said Little Jack.

"Why don't you go with Bunnikin?" asked Granpa.
"Are Bunnikins invited?" asked Little Jack Rabbit.
"Oh, yes," said Granpa, "I should think so, Little
Jack. I should think Bunnikins are invited."
So Little Jack Rabbit put on his
smart new jacket and his
shiny new shoes …

and he went to the party
with Bunnikin.

Little Jack Rabbit held on to Bunnikin. He played *What's the Time, Mr Wolf?* and *Pop Goes the Weasel!* But when he tried to play *Pass the Parcel* he had to leave Bunnikin on the ground –

and when he came back, what did he find …

but a teddy sitting next to Bunnikin.

The teddy belonged to Rosy.

"I've never been to a party before," said Rosy.

"Is that why you brought Teddy?" asked Little
Jack Rabbit.

"Yes," said Rosy.

"I brought Bunnikin," said Little Jack.

"I think Teddy likes Bunnikin," said Rosy.

"Bunnikin likes Teddy," said Little Jack.

"Perhaps we should leave them together," said
Rosy. "Come on, let's go and have some tea."

After tea little Jack Rabbit had such fun playing
with his new friend Rosy, he didn't want to go
home when Granpa came to fetch him.
"Don't forget Bunnikin, Little Jack," said Granpa.

It had been a big day for Little Jack Rabbit. He had been to his first party.

"I'm going to another party soon," said Little Jack.

"Oh," said Mummy.

"It's Rosy's party," said Little Jack.

"Can I come with you?" asked Mummy.

"No," said Little Jack.

"But I'm your mummy," said Mummy.

"Mummies aren't invited," said Little Jack Rabbit.

"Good night, Little Jack," said Mummy.

MORE WALKER PAPERBACKS
For You to Enjoy

OH, LITTLE JACK
by Inga Moore

In this first story about Little Jack Rabbit and his family, the young bunny seems to be too small for everything, until his grandfather saves the day!

"A classic… A real pleasure to read aloud." *Parents*

0-7445-3126-8   £3.99

FIFTY RED NIGHT-CAPS
by Inga Moore

This amusing, surprising and delightfully illustrated retelling of a traditional story, depicts the adventure of a boy taking a bag of night-caps to sell at the market and the troupe of playful monkeys he meets in the forest.

0-7445-1783-4   £3.99

AWAY IN A MANGER
by Sarah Hayes / Inga Moore

The Nativity story seen through the eyes of its supporting characters, with the words of six favourite carols.

"Original and informative… Rich, traditional pictures." *The Independent*

0-7445-1326-X   £3.99